Sinbad

and the Ogre

by Martin Waddell and O'Kif

FRANKLIN WATTS

LONDON•SYDNEY

First published in 2009 by
Franklin Watts
338 Euston Road
London
NW1 3BH

Franklin Watts Australia
Level 17/207 Kent Street
Sydney
NSW 2000

A CIP catalogue record for this book is available
from the British Library.

ISBN 978 0 7496 8559 1 (hbk)
ISBN 978 0 7496 8571 3 (pbk)

Series Editor: Jackie Hamley
Series Advisor: Dr Barrie Wade
Series Designer: Peter Scoulding

Printed in China

Franklin Watts is a division of
Hachette Children's Books,
an Hachette UK company
www.hachette.co.uk

Sinbad the Sailor often
sailed into trouble.

One day, Sinbad's ship ran into a terrible storm. The crew had to swim to a nearby island.

"That was a lucky escape!"
cried Sinbad.

Then they were captured by
ogres and held as prisoners!

"They'll eat us for sure,"
sobbed the ship's captain.
"No one's eating me," Sinbad told
Ali, his friend. "We must escape!"

7

An ogre as tall as a palm tree
appeared. He was the chief.
The others were only shrub-size,
but just as nasty.

The huge ogre had one wild,
red eye in his forehead and
large, dripping jaws.

9

"Supper!" gloated the huge
ogre, picking up Sinbad.
"You don't want to eat me.
I'm too thin," Sinbad said.

"Fat would be better," agreed
the huge ogre as he looked at
the captain. "You will make
a better meal!"

The small ogres popped the
captain in the pot. They cooked
him with rice, lightly sprinkled
with minced ship's cat for flavour.

"Fatten the rest of them up!"
ordered the huge ogre.
"The less we eat, the longer we'll
live!" Sinbad whispered to Ali.

The small ogres fed the crew
all day long. The crew grew fatter
and fatter each day, while Sinbad
and Ali grew thinner and thinner.

The ogres enjoyed their dinners. Soon there were only a few sailors left, including Sinbad and Ali.

• MONDAY •
CREW STEW
• TUESDAY •
LEG OF MATE WITH
SAILOR SAUCE
• WEDNESDAY •
CABIN BOY CURRY
CHEF'S CHOICE OF
VEGETABLES WITH
ALL DISHES
• PUDDING •
ICED SCREAM

"Save us, Sinbad!" pleaded
the chubby sailors.
"How do we get out of this?"
groaned Ali.

"Think, think, THINK!" Sinbad
said, gritting his teeth.
And he thought...

And he thought...

18

"One in the eye for the chief!"
grinned Sinbad.

That night, Sinbad and Ali
slipped through the fences
down to the shore.

They made a raft and
sharpened some sticks.

Then Sinbad and Ali crept
back into the ogres' camp.

"Do what I do!" Sinbad
told the sailors.

"NOW!" yelled Sinbad.

"ARGH!"

roared the huge ogre.

24

"**HELP!**" the small ogres screeched as the huge ogre lumbered blindly among them. "Follow me!" yelled Sinbad.

"No treasure this time, Sinbad!"
the sailors joked as they sailed
home on their raft.

"Sad, but true," sighed Sinbad.
But when they got back to port,
Sinbad had another plan.

Sinbad and Ali broke up the
raft and sold off the pieces.

Sinbad soon made lots of money,
and so did his friend Ali!

Puzzle 1

Put these pictures in the correct order.
Which event do you think is most important?
Now try writing the story in your own words!

Puzzle 2

1. Which of us will be next?

2. I'll get us out of this mess!

3. Yum! Sailor supper!

4. Help! Save us from the cooking pot!

5. We need to find more sticks.

6. Feed them up so they make a good meal!

Choose the correct speech bubbles for the characters above. Can you think of any others? Turn over to find the answers.

Answers

Puzzle 1

The correct order is: 1f, 2a, 3c, 4b, 5e, 6d

Puzzle 2

Sinbad: 2, 5

The sailors: 1, 4

The ogre: 3, 6

Look out for more Hopscotch Adventures:

TALES OF KING ARTHUR

1. The Sword in the Stone
ISBN 978 0 7496 6694 1

2. Arthur the King
ISBN 978 0 7496 6695 8

3. The Round Table
ISBN 978 0 7496 6697 2

4. Sir Lancelot and the Ice Castle
ISBN 978 0 7496 6698 9

5. Sir Gawain and the Green Knight
ISBN 978 0 7496 8557 7*
ISBN 978 0 7496 8569 0

6. Sir Galahad and the Holy Grail
ISBN 978 0 7496 8558 4*
ISBN 978 0 7496 8570 6

TALES OF ROBIN HOOD

Robin and the Knight
ISBN 978 0 7496 6699 6

Robin and the Monk
ISBN 978 0 7496 6700 9

Robin and the Silver Arrow
ISBN 978 0 7496 6703 0

Robin and the Friar
ISBN 978 0 7496 6702 3

Robin and the Butcher
ISBN 978 0 7496 8555 3*
ISBN 978 0 7496 8568 3

Robin and Maid Marian
ISBN 978 0 7496 8556 0*
ISBN 978 0 7496 8567 6

TALES OF SINBAD THE SAILOR

Sinbad and the Ogre
ISBN 978 0 7496 8559 1*
ISBN 978 0 7496 8571 3

Sinbad and the Whale
ISBN 978 0 7496 8553 9*
ISBN 978 0 7496 8565 2

Sinbad and the Diamond Valley
ISBN 978 0 7496 8554 6*
ISBN 978 0 7496 8566 9

Sinbad and the Monkeys
ISBN 978 0 7496 8560 7*
ISBN 978 0 7496 8572 0

For more Hopscotch Adventures and other Hopscotch stories, visit:
www.franklinwatts.co.uk

* hardback